Librarian Reviewer
Joanne Bongaarts
Educational Consultant
MS in Library Media Education, Minnesota State University, Mankato
Teacher and Media Specialist with Edina Public Schools, MN, 1993–2000

Reading Consultant
Elizabeth Stedem
Educator/Consultant, Colorado Springs, CO
MA in Elementary Education, University of Denver, CO

First published in the United States in 2007
by Stone Arch Books,
151 Good Counsel Drive, P.O. Box 669,
Mankato, Minnesota 56002.
www.stonearchbooks.com

First published by Evans Brothers Ltd,
2A Portman Mansions, Chiltern Street,
London W1U 6NR, United Kingdom.

Library of Congress Cataloging-in-Publication Data
Lawrie, Robin.
    First Among Losers / by Robin and Chris Lawrie; illustrated by
Robin Lawrie.
    p. cm. — (Ridge Riders)
    Summary: Slam Duncan and his fellow mountain bikers, having just
learned how to ride the giant jump, the Dragon, are now determined to
out-jump their arch-rival, Punk Tuer, whose bike has a secret weapon.
    ISBN-13: 978-1-59889-125-6 (library binding)
    ISBN-10: 1-59889-125-1 (library binding)
    ISBN-13: 978-1-59889-273-4 (paperback)
    ISBN-10: 1-59889-273-8 (paperback)
    [1. All terrain cycling—Fiction. 2. Bicycle racing—Fiction.] I.
Lawrie, Christine. II. Title. III. Series: Lawrie, Robin. Ridge Riders.
PZ7.L438218Fir 2007
[Fic]—dc22   2006005967

1 2 3 4 5 6 11 10 09 08 07 06

FIRST AMONG LOSERS

by Robin and Chris Lawrie
illustrated by Robin Lawrie

ᵥᵥ STONE ARCH BOOKS
MINNEAPOLIS   SAN DIEGO

The Ridge Riders

 Hi, my name is "Slam" Duncan.

This is Aziz. We call him Dozy.

Then there's Larry.

This is Fiona.

And Andy.

* I'm Andy. (Andy is deaf. He uses sign language instead of talking.)

We call ourselves the Ridge Riders.
We practice and race on a hill called
Westridge behind the town where we
live. Some property developers want
to put houses on it. They want to
build right over our favorite courses,
so we made a new one on the other
side of the hill.

Our new course goes over an old rock quarry, so we had to build lots of aerial rampways and flyovers to cross the rough ground.

One of the toughest jumps is
called "The Dragon." Someone
stuck teeth shapes in it, and
old headlights for eyes.
That makes it even scarier.

If you don't get it just right,

you could have a hard landing.
To avoid problems like this, the
Ridge Riders were training together.
We wanted to be ready for
the next race.

Brake before the drop.

Pre-jump here.

Keep your front wheel up here.

Lean back here.

8

Our main rival, Punk Tuer, was training with a bunch of riders who never helped each other.

But, of course, Punk doesn't need to do much training. He can win races just by having the very newest bike technology.

His dad owns a store, Tuer Bikes.
So whenever Punk missed a landing . . .

Then his "friends" would move in.

They knew how to do that, all right.
They were quite happy to see Punk keep
wrecking bikes.

As we kept practicing the Dragon, the Ridge Riders' jumps got better and better — and Punk's got worse and worse. Suddenly a group of cross-country riders came whooshing by.

One of the riders had a blowout. For some reason, Punk and his crew thought this was very funny.

But their laughter stopped soon, when the cross-country rider 1) pulled the old tube out, 2) zapped a new one in, then pulled a tiny compressed air cartridge out of his pocket, and 3) stuck it in the valve.

Instant inflation!

Awesome. Even Punk's dad seemed impressed.
That night I saw the mechanics at Tuer Cycles
working late.

The next day, everyone was back on the hill, training hard. Everyone except Larry, who was digging around in the dirt.

We all crowded around to get a better look.

I thought it was pretty boring, so I picked up Larry's binoculars.

Looking through binoculars the wrong way is really cool. Everything looks like it's very far away. You feel really alone. Even all the other downhillers seemed to be gone. Except for Punk, who was coming toward me, but he was miles away. Or so I thought.

PPHHHwAPP!

It was the biggest jump we had ever seen!

So, what did you think of that? Tire-inflation cylinders connected to the pressure valves of front and back tires controlled by a switch.

The following Saturday was the start of the two-day race weekend. We knew Punk would be using his compressed-air jumping system, so after our first runs we met up at the Dragon to check out Punk's run.

The front cylinder worked, but the rear one didn't. Result: A loop-de-loop, another smashed bike, and a mad Punk.

On our way to lunch, we couldn't help overhearing the conversation between Punk and his dad in their van.

Dozy had to leave after lunch to help out at his family's grocery store in town. Later, he told me what happened that afternoon.

Okay, Dozy! You do sports psychology for your weird bunch of Ridge Riders misfits. You can do it for me. Here, how much do you want for it? I've got tons of cash!

Sorry, Punk. I only work for the Ridge Riders. But my Uncle Deepak's a pretty good therapist. I'll give him a call and tell him we're coming over.

Hmmphh! He better be good!

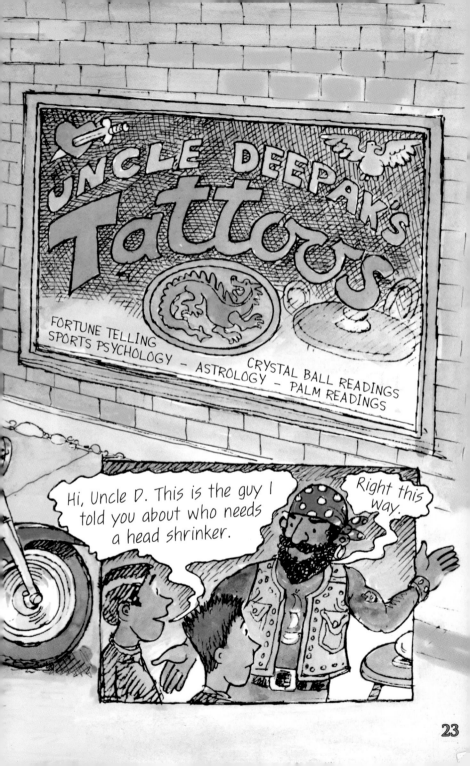

Uncle Deepak got out his crystal ball.

I can see somebody who thinks he can buy friends. I see someone who doesn't know the meaning of **"teamwork."**

Then he showed Punk one of his most popular tattoos.

This is the teamwork tattoo.

It shows a dragon crushing a warrior. He relied too much on heavy armor and weaponry. Quick, lightweight warriors pin it down by working as a team.

Next, Uncle Deepak did a ball-point tattoo on Punk's arm to remind him to find some real friends.

That evening, Larry, Andy, and I were getting in some last-minute training before the next day's race. We had done okay in the first race, but we hadn't won. And who should appear but . . .

Suddenly he seemed to want to be friends.

Listen, Punk. How come suddenly you're all friendly? What do you want?

Well, because I need somebody to show me how to jump the Dragon.

I should've known. Why should I help you? Get out of here.

But Andy wasn't happy about my bad behavior. He signed to me that I was trying to find an easy victory. He also reminded me that Punk was trying to be friends. I thought about what he told me.

27

Andy was right,
and I knew it. If I
beat someone who
wasn't good, then I would
be an only-slightly-less-than-bad winner.
First among losers.
I yelled, "Hey, Punk!"

I could see his problem right away!

He was roaring off the cliff,
like a bag of cement
on wheels, instead
of pre-jumping it.

Okay, Punk. Here's what you've got to do. **(1)** Five feet from the edge, push down hard on the pedals and handlebars, compressing the springs. **(2)** As you get close to the edge, let the springs rebound while you pull up. That's a pre-jump. It'll give you tons of extra height.

Punk learned fast. Soon, he conquered
the Dragon.

Sunday morning, race two, first run. Punk would be the last one down, so after our runs we all met at the Dragon to watch. Uncle Deepak and his friends were already there.

Even the Ridge Riders
cheered for him.

The landing was perfect.

But I still beat him!

About the Author and Illustrator

Robin and Chris Lawrie wrote the *Ridge Riders* books together, and Robin illustrated them. Their inspiration for these books is their son. They wanted to write books that he would find interesting. Many of the *Ridge Riders* books are based on adventures he and his friends had while biking. Robin and Chris live in England, and will soon be moving to a big, old house that is also home to sixty bats.

Glossary

aerial (AIR-ee-uhl)—reaching high into the air

compressing (kuhm-PRESS-ing)—pressing together or squeezing

deaf (DEF)—not being able to hear well or to hear at all

head shrinker (HED SHRINGK-ur)—slang for a psychiatrist, a person who helps you with your attitude or feelings about life

psychology (sye-KOL-uh-jist)—the science that deals with mental habits and behavior

technology (tek-NOL-uh-jee)—scientific knowledge

therapist (THER-uh-pist)—one who treats an illness or disability

valve (VALV)—a small part on a tube or pipe that controls the flow of air

Internet Sites

Do you want to know more about subjects related to this book? Or are you interested in learning about other topics? Then check out FactHound, a fun, easy way to find Internet sites.

Our investigative staff has already sniffed out great sites for you!

Here's how to use FactHound:

1. Visit *www.facthound.com*

2. Select your grade level.

3. To learn more about subjects related to this book, type in the book's ISBN number: **1598891251**.

4. Click the **Fetch It** button.

FactHound will fetch the best Internet sites for you!

Discussion Questions

1. When you first read the title of this story, what did you think it meant? Now that you've read the story, what does it mean to you? Discuss your thinking.

2. Why, on the last page, does Uncle Deepak think that Slam needs a head shrinker? (Head shrinker is another name for a therapist or psychologist—a person who studies how people behave and why). Does Slam need someone to "shrink his head"? Why or why not?

3. Even the Ridge Riders cheered for Punk's jump at the end of the story. How do you think Punk felt when they did that?

Writing Prompts

1. The phrase "to slay the dragon" is used often to describe a person overcoming a challenge. (In this story, Punk conquers a jump called "The Dragon.") Write about a challenge that you have faced and what you did to overcome it. Be sure to include your feelings as well as what happened.

2. Punk learns how to jump the Dragon by asking for Slam's help. He and Slam were never friends before. Are there people you would like to be friends with, and maybe learn from? Tell us what they are like, and how they make you feel.

Read other adventures of the Ridge Riders

Cheat Challenge

Slam Duncan and his friends, the Ridge Riders, don't know what to think when they come across a sword buried deep in their mountain-biking course. It's part of a new racing course contest called Excalibur. Then Slam accidentally gets a look at the map of the course, but he knows he can't tell his teammates the map's secrets.

Fear 3.1

While rock climbing, Slam loses his foothold. Luckily, his safety harness holds, but that doesn't stop Slam from being terrified. Soon, he can't even manage to complete the mountain biking courses he's ridden on for years. Will Slam ever get over his fear?

Snow Bored

The Ridge Riders are bored. So much snow has fallen on their mountain biking practice hill that they can't ride. Luckily, Dozy has a great idea. He turns an old skateboard and a pair of sneakers into a snowboard. Before long, everyone is snowboarding.

White Lightning

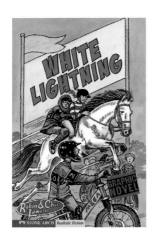

Someone smashed the Ridge Riders' practice jumps, and they suspect Fiona and her horse-riding friends. The boys are so mean to Fiona that she leaves. Then Slam gets a flat tire and has to race back home to get his spare, and he only has 50 minutes! Now a horse would come in handy!

Check out Stone Arch Books graphic novels!

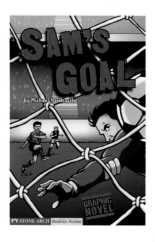

Sam's Goal
Michael Hardcastle

When England's top goal-scorer invites Sam to his next soccer game, he can't believe it. The problem is, neither do Sam's friends.

The Haunted Surfboard
Anthony Masters

The only good thing about Jack's new school is that it's near the ocean and he loves to surf. Then Jack meets Peter, a daredevil who insists on risking his life every time he enters the water.